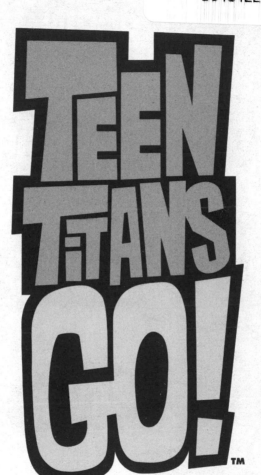

TEEN TITANS GO!

CYBORG CIRCUIT OVERLOAD

Adapted by **J. E. Bright**

Based on the episodes
"Oil Drums" written by **Michael Jelenic**
and **Aaron Horvath**
"Slumber Party" written by **Ben Joseph**
and
"Real Boy Adventures" written by **Ben Joseph**

LITTLE, BROWN AND COMPANY
New York Boston

Little, Brown and Company

Hachette Book Group
1290 Avenue of the Americas, New York, NY 10104
Visit us at lb-kids.com

Little, Brown and Company is a division of
Hachette Book Group, Inc.
The Little, Brown name and logo are trademarks of
Hachette Book Group, Inc.

First Edition: April 2015

ISBN 978-0-316-33336-8

Library of Congress Control Number: 2015930156

10 9 8 7 6 5 4 3 2

RRD-C

Printed in the United States of America

CONTENTS

CHAPTER 1

Cyborg rushed into the modern living room of Titans Tower to find his teammates, Robin, Raven, Beast Boy, and Starfire, strewn all over the couch.

"Oh, yeah!" Cyborg cheered, holding up a few metallic fingers. "I've got three letters for you tonight."

"BLT?" guessed Robin. He'd been craving the sandwich all day.

Beast Boy perked up. "VIP?" he asked.

"UFO?" suggested Starfire.

"LOL," said Raven. She didn't smile.

"No, no, no, and no," replied Cyborg. "They are…" He counted the letters on his fingers. "*V. H.* And *S.*" He showed them a box filled with antique videotapes. "That's right. I got VHSes for days!"

Cyborg grinned when he saw the other Titans' eyes shine with excitement.

"Can we watch *The Silver Sisters?*" asked Raven. "I love those sassy old broads."

Starfire floated off the couch. "I would like to watch the *Pudding Half Hour Show of Sweaters.*"

"Let's watch *Furry Alien Thing* again," Robin growled. "I love *Furry Alien Thing*." Robin's expression became blank and distant. "Yes," he whispered to the alien in his imagination. "Eat that cat, Furry Alien Thing. Eat him. He's hiding in the kitchen drawer, Furry Alien Thing. But be patient. Savor the hunt, you beast…"

Cyborg shook his half-metal head. "Those are all great shows, but tonight we are watching… *The B-Squad*!"

"*B* is the second highest of letters," said Starfire. "It must be good!"

Cyborg's mechanical eye glowed as he hugged *The B-Squad* VHS tape. "It's about four cool dudes who ride in a van...with a stripe!"

"I love stripes," said Robin. "Is it red?"

"You know it's red," replied Cyborg. "And they protect the innocent from bad guys!"

"Oh," said Raven. She blinked once. "Kind of like us."

"Except they aren't lame," said Cyborg while plugging the VCR into the Titans' huge TV. "They make cool weapons out of junk, like oil drums and pieces of discarded metal."

Transforming into a green panther, Beast Boy flipped onto his back over the couch arm and lay limply as if on a tree limb. "That sounds so awesome!"

"It is," agreed Cyborg. He pushed *The B-Squad* tape into the VCR. "Now let's get this party started!"

He stared at the snarled mess of electronics, wires, gadgets, and gizmos under the TV.

"Uh…" he said. "Where's the remote?"

CHAPTER 2

Cyborg's teammates shrugged on the couch.

"I don't know," said Robin.

Starfire's bright green eyes peered around. "I have not seen the remote control," she said.

"Beats me," said Beast Boy.

Raven made a noise to indicate that she didn't know and didn't quite care.

Cyborg swallowed his worried feelings. "It's probably just in the couch cushions," he said. He pushed between the other Titans and dug into the space in the corner of the cushions, jamming his hand within the crevice.

As he burrowed, he pulled out lots of lost items. He grabbed handfuls of coins, which he tossed over his shoulder.

Beast Boy turned into a sea lion and dove after the change, collecting each coin and spinning them on his nose.

Then Cyborg discovered an old chicken leg, an apple core, a slice of old pizza with a big bite in the side…and some gross goo that nobody could identify.

"Ew," said Raven.

With no sign of the remote control, Cyborg tunneled deeper into the couch, his mechanical arms searching so quickly they started to blur. Bits of gunk and fluff and junk flew out like confetti. Cyborg kicked his feet in the air as his head and body disappeared into the world beneath the couch cushions.

Then Cyborg suddenly sat up, his robot eye flashing in alarm, his human eye wide with concern. "It's not here," he breathed. His voice rose sharply. "The remote is not here!"

Robin patted his teammate on his metal shoulder. "Hey, it's okay, Cyborg," he said. "We can just use the buttons on the TV."

"The buttons?" said Cyborg. His expression calmed, and he smiled brightly. "The buttons!

You're right. The TV's got all sorts of buttons for things."

The whole team rushed over to the TV, tilting their heads at its controls.

There were hundreds of buttons on the TV's lower panel, in all shapes and sizes and colors, along with switches and connectors and pins and a bewildering array of tiny doohickeys and doodads. It looked more complicated than the controls of an intergalactic spaceship.

Cyborg waggled his finger over the various buttons. There didn't seem to be any labels for the controls, or if there were, they might have been in an alien language or some kind of code.

With a cry of defeat, Cyborg gave up trying to figure out the buttons. He collapsed in a heap on the floor in front of the TV. His shoulders shuddered with sobs.

"Would you relax?" scolded Raven. She hovered a few inches off the ground by Cyborg's head. "The remote will turn up eventually. We'll watch *The B-Squad* some other time."

Cyborg sat back on his heels. "This is not about *The B-Squad*," he wailed. "Or *Chuckie Says* or *Merriam* or *Little Girl Robot* or *Wooden Spoons* or *Mustache, Private Detective* or *Cousin from Unknown Island* or *Jolly Hours*—"

"Cyborg," Raven replied, "gimme a break."

"Without TV," Cyborg whispered, tears streaming down his face, "I don't know what to do with myself."

Robin tapped his knuckles against his friend's steel skull. "It's just TV, Cyborg," he said.

"*Just* TV?" cried Cyborg. "The best moments of my life have been sitting in front of that guy. TV has taught me life lessons, made me laugh, and filled lots of empty time."

"Wow," Robin said, rubbing his chin. "You sound like a crazy person. I think we should use this opportunity to take a break from TV."

In unison, Cyborg, Raven, Starfire, and Beast Boy gasped in horror.

CHAPTER 3

"What?" shouted Cyborg. **"Why would** we want to do *that*?"

Robin crossed his arms and scowled. "Because concerned parents have theorized for decades that TV rots the brain."

Cyborg crossed his arms, too. "Well, that's obviously ridiculous," he said. "TV keeps your brain active, healthy, and strong!"

Poking his head up between the two as a concerned-looking antelope, Beast Boy told Cyborg, "I don't know, dude. If a parent said it, it has to be true."

Robin nodded. "Then instead of watching TV," he decided, "we're going to spend our time hanging out with one another."

"Yay!" cried Starfire, Beast Boy, and Raven. Starfire threw her hands in the air in celebration.

Cyborg didn't look too sure about the idea at all.

The next hour was the slowest of the Teen Titans' entire lives.

They gathered around the kitchen table and sat there stupefied with boredom, staring at a big clock on the wall. Its hands seemed frozen still.

"Without TV," muttered Raven, "you really notice how long every second is."

Everybody kept watching the clock. The second hand wiggled tensely, struggling to move, then finally ticked.

"Are you serious?" hollered Cyborg. "How many more of those are there before we go to sleep?"

"Approximately thirty-two thousand," replied Starfire.

"I am not doing this thirty-two thousand more times!" yelled Cyborg.

Robin stood and put his hands flat on the table. "All right," he said. "We need an activity to occupy our time. Let's engage in some meaningful conversation."

Beast Boy turned into a sea turtle and tilted his head at Robin. "How do you meaningfully conversate, bro?"

"We just express our thoughts and feelings with words," Robin explained.

"Thoughts," said Beast Boy, nodding his head.

Raven said, "Hmmm."

"Feelings," said Starfire. She scratched the side of her arm. "Yes, all right."

"Great," said Robin. "I'll start. Um…" He stared at the center of the table, concentrating.

"Good afternoon," he said awkwardly. "This is a nice day. For things."

Nobody knew how to reply to that, so they all shifted in their chairs, staying quiet for too long.

"Hi," said Beast Boy, finally breaking the silence. "I'm a person."

Cyborg nodded thoughtfully. "I know when I do things."

"One time," said Starfire, "I saw…"

Raven slumped her head down onto the table. "Eeehhhhh," she moaned.

"You guys remember," Robin prompted, "things…"

Cyborg shook his finger in the air. "So fun when we…Right?"

All five Titans laughed heartily, as if remembering fantastic adventures in the past. Then their laughter trailed off into nervous, awkward giggles and fizzled out altogether into dismayed quiet.

Cyborg stood and let out a shriek. "We have to find the remote and watch TV!" he screamed. "Now!"

CHAPTER 4

"**Don't panic, Titans,**" Robin said, staring at each of his teammates through his mask. "We just have to do whatever people did for fun before TV."

The five teenagers pondered that. Starfire raised her hand, as though she had an idea, but then she lowered it again.

Beast Boy turned into an owl, and then

back into his green human form. "Like…" he suggested, "a parade?"

His friends nodded slowly, not quite sure. "Oh," said Raven, "I've heard of those."

Before any of the Titans even had time to think about it, they found a parade and watched marchers and floats from the crowded sidelines behind a wooden police barrier. Streamers wriggled down from the sky and cheers erupted all around.

None of the Titans looked impressed.

Cyborg pointed at the marching in the street. "This is a parade?" he complained.

"It's just people walking," growled Robin.

"And why are the automobiles traveling so slowly?" asked Starfire. "Is it deliberate to make it the boring?"

When they heard the sounds of tubas, trombones, and trumpets, Beast Boy covered his ears. "Don't tell me that's another marching band!" he whined, cringing. "It's just marching band after marching band after marching band!"

Then a muscular male cheerleader appeared, twirling a silver baton. He spun the glittery stick into the air and caught it with a flourish.

Raven smiled. "Whoa," she said. "Look at him spin that baton." She watched for another split second. "Okay, I'm over it."

All together, the Teen Titans cupped their hands around their mouths and bellowed, "Booooo!"

Back in the kitchen of Titans Tower, the teammates sat around the table feeling even more dejected than they had before the parade.

"I can't," moaned Cyborg. "I can't take any more parades or terrible conversations. Let's just find the remote and watch *Crime, He Said*."

"That's going to rot your brain, Cyborg," argued Robin. "Instead, let's use these new seconds we have to pursue fulfilling activities that enrich our lives." He nudged Beast Boy. "Haven't you always wanted to learn how to play the keyboard?"

"Don't have the time, bro," said Beast Boy.

"Now you do," replied Robin. "And Raven, haven't you always wanted to be a bodybuilder?"

"No," said Raven.

"Now you can!" continued Robin. He smiled at Starfire. "Star, you've always wanted to do volunteer work for the poor but didn't want to miss your favorite shows."

Starfire rubbed her fingers, worrying. "There are so many of the poor people but even more of the shows to watch."

Robin stood up and opened his arms wide. "Now we can all follow our passions, because without TV we have nothing better to do," he declared. He held up a fist. "Titans, *go!*"

In a rush, the Teen Titans got busy.

Beast Boy practiced playing a big electronic keyboard.

Raven pumped iron.

Cooking a complicated omelet, Cyborg made a mess in the kitchen.

Teaching himself to build furniture, Robin hammered legs onto a chair.

Ladling out food to hungry people, Starfire volunteered at a soup kitchen.

Then the teammates gathered outside the Tower. Together, they hopped on a long bicycle built for five and pedaled happily around their Tower, cheering their newfound leisure time.

In the afternoon, Starfire and Raven lounged around the living room, resting on the comfortable furniture Robin had built. In the background, Beast Boy had turned into an octopus to play a complicated piece on his keyboard.

Wearing a chef's hat, Cyborg entered, carrying a tray of small plates of food. He placed it down on the coffee table. "Who wants tapas?" he asked.

Starfire tasted a morsel of food. "Mmm," she said. "My friends at the kitchen of soup would love this recipe!"

Raven chewed a bite of Cyborg's dish. "Great source of protein," she said.

Beast Boy turned into a green tiger. "You said it," he agreed.

Robin smiled proudly at his friends. "Look at us, Titans," he said, getting emotional. "We did it. We filled time!"

"So many seconds went by!" cheered Beast Boy.

Everybody fell silent as they stared down at the food. Their hands and shoulders twitched.

Raven shook her head sadly. "So why do we feel so empty inside?" she asked.

CHAPTER 5

Cyborg bowed his head and clasped his hands together. "Maybe we feel empty inside because..." He peered up at Beast Boy. "Because learning to play the keyboard did not teach you about friendship." He waved at Starfire. "And volunteering did not make you a better person." Cyborg frowned at Raven. "And there's nothing funny about bodybuilding."

Raven flexed an overly developed bicep. "You can say that again," she said, her voice disturbingly deep.

The other Titans nodded their heads, agreeing with Cyborg.

"Only TV can give us those things," Cyborg concluded. "Life without TV is meaningless. The Teen Titans are supposed to be heroes, but the real hero is television. Can I get a 'turn it on?'"

"Turn it on!" the Titans chanted.

Beast Boy transformed into a beagle. He raised his green snout and took a big sniff. "Hey," he said, "what's that smell?"

The other Titans inhaled. They sniffed the air, too.

Cyborg pinched his nostrils shut. "Oh,

that's not right," he groaned.

"Ew," said Raven.

"Yeah," Robin agreed.

Starfire stifled a gag. "I do not understand," she moaned.

"No, no, no!" Cyborg cried in alarm. He grabbed Robin's head in both metal hands and took a big whiff of the Boy Wonder's skull. "This is bad." Cyborg pushed Robin out of the way and smelled Starfire's head. He shuddered. "Your brains," he said, his human eye wide and his robot eye flashing. "They're rotting!"

"But we haven't been watching TV," argued Raven.

"Exactly," Cyborg replied. "Just as I suspected, TV keeps your brain from rotting by feeding it information and good times."

Beast Boy, still a beagle, sniffed Cyborg's partially metal skull. "But your brain doesn't stink."

Cyborg smiled. "It's because I've watched so much quality programming my brain is stronger than yours."

Robin stood in a heroic pose, one fist raised. "Then the rest of us need to get in front of a TV before our brains rot away completely!"

"But," said Starfire, "the device that controls remotely is still missing."

Cyborg put his hands on his hips. "Then we improvise," he said. "Just like the B-Squad."

Moments later, Cyborg blasted inspiring music in the work shed of Titans Tower while he rolled an empty oil drum over to his tool bench. He tightened a nut on the drum with a wrench. Then he flipped a safety visor down over his human eye and welded a seam with a fiery torch. He grinned as glowing bits of molten metal sprayed around the work shed.

When he was finished, he carried his creation upstairs to show it off. "I love when a plan comes together," he bragged to his teammates.

Out of the oil drum, Cyborg had fashioned a large, empty television frame.

Robin and the other Titans stared skeptically. "What plan?" Robin asked. "That's not a TV."

"Just look," replied Cyborg. He picked up the empty TV frame, and held it in front of a straggly potted begonia that needed watering. "It's a show about plants."

The other Titans smiled as they got the idea.

"This is just as good as anything on TV," said Robin.

"Oooh," said Beast Boy, "can we change the channel?" He turned into a fat warthog, and then quickly into an elegant border collie. "I want to watch something else."

"No problem!" replied Cyborg. He carried the TV frame over to a dusty corner of the room, where three bugs scuttled into the shadows. "How about *The Cockroach Show*?"

Raven stuck out her tongue, grossed out. "I want to watch the show about Wall," she said.

"Which one are you talking about, Rave?" Cyborg asked, confused.

"You know," said Raven. "The one about Wall."

"Oh, right!" said Cyborg cheerfully. "*The Wall Show*!" He held up the TV frame in front of an empty patch of wall.

Raven nodded and smiled.

"Huh," said Robin, watching *The Wall Show*. "Is that stain new or from the last episode?"

"I think it's new," replied Cyborg. Then

a nasty bug crawled across the wall. "Look! It's a crossover episode from *The Cockroach Show*."

As Starfire floated backward, Raven sniffed her teammate's long curly hair. "The smell's getting worse," she reported.

Robin tightened his hands into fists. "It's not working, Cyborg," he said.

Cyborg grimaced. He quickly shifted the TV frame so it showed a slice of pizza lying on the table. "How about now?" he asked.

The other Titans sniffed. They wrinkled their noses in disgust. A greenish cloud of stinky odor wafted around their heads.

Cyborg pointed at them, terrified. "Your brains!" he screamed. "They've completely rotted!"

CHAPTER 6

Starfire's green eyes became blank. She raised her arms out in front of her. "It is so… nice out…" she moaned like a zombie.

"Let's go…for a hike…" groaned Robin, shuffling from side to side.

Beast Boy turned into a green zombie. "Join us," he croaked to Cyborg, "for a game…of miniature golf…bro."

Raven moaned and groaned, too. "I'm taking...a French class," she whimpered. *"Zut alors!"*

"Your rotted brains are making you crazy!" Cyborg screeched. He stepped backward, scared out of his wits, until his back hit the wall.

Grunting and sighing, Robin, Starfire, Beast Boy, and Raven shuffled toward him.

"No!" hollered Cyborg, blocking his face with his arms. "No, I don't want to do activities! You can't make me!"

Even with his face covered, Cyborg saw an intense flash of light shine throughout the room. He lowered his arms enough to see his teammates staggering backward from the surprising power of the mystery glow.

Cyborg gasped when he saw that the

big-screen TV, now completely alive, had stepped off the wall and onto the console. It had wiry arms and legs and a big droopy mustache. The TV seemed to be wearing the tiniest shorts Cyborg had ever seen.

"TV?" asked Cyborg, amazed. "What are you doing here?"

The television turned its forceful glow toward Cyborg. "I have raised countless children, Cyborg," the TV said, "but you have always been my favorite. You might be surprised to know that all those years you spent staring at me, I was staring right back at you. It's been a joy to help shape you into the man you are today. I love you, Cyborg."

A tear trailed down the human side of Cyborg's face. "I love you, too, TV," he whispered.

The TV put an arm around Cyborg's shoulders. "Now the only way to save your friends is to reverse their brain rot with quality programming."

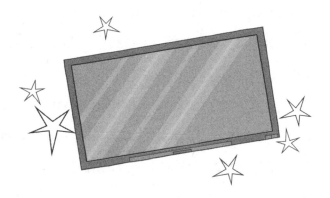

Cyborg twisted to gesture at the TV's glowing blank screen. "Turn yourself on, dude!" he said.

The TV peered down at its own insanely complicated control panel. It shrugged. "I don't know how these buttons work," it said. "No one does. Where's the remote?"

"We lost it," Cyborg said, hanging his head. "It could be anywhere."

The TV raised a fist. "Then we're going to have to find it. Let's go!"

Cyborg nodded, and he and the TV zoomed around, searching for the remote. First they inspected every nook and cranny of Titans Tower, but they couldn't find the remote anywhere. So they tooled around the neighborhood in a classic detective's car on patrol. They interrogated a shifty suspect, who gave them a hot tip.

That lead helped the TV and Cyborg track down a dirty bad guy, whom they chased, siren blaring and tires squealing, back to his hideout.

The bad guy was keeping the remote hostage in a filthy warehouse! So the TV and Cyborg rescued the remote and escaped across the harbor on a speedboat while the hideout exploded dramatically behind them.

When Cyborg and the TV got back to Titans Tower, they were attacked by Cyborg's zombified teammates.

Before the brainwashed Titans could grab Cyborg, he raised the remote control.

Cyborg pressed the On button.

The TV froze in place against the wall. Its screen lit up with a high-definition picture.

The zombified Titans ceased their shuffling steps. Their blank eyes whirled as they stared at the show on the TV's screen.

Raven, Beast Boy, Robin, and Starfire rubbed their swelling heads as their brains restored to normal in the healing glow of the television. Their eyes returned to normal and they stopped moaning. Instead, they smiled at the TV.

Robin blinked hard twice. "Thanks for fixing our brains, TV," he said.

"No problem," the TV replied. "So…I was thinking, it's such a beautiful day. Why don't we all go on a hike? Or perhaps take in some culture at a museum?"

The teenage heroes glanced at one another with worried expressions on their faces.

The TV laughed. "I'm just messing with you," it said. "Let's watch hours of *The B-Squad*!"

With a big, happy cheer, the Teen Titans jumped into the air, pumping their fists in celebration.

CHAPTER 1

One night, Cyborg arrived back at Titans Tower, exhausted from a long day of protecting the innocent. He yawned as he plodded into his room.

"Bedtime," he said with a weary sigh. "Lights out."

Cyborg flipped the wall switch and the room went dark.

"And night-light on," said Cyborg.

He clicked on the night-light that was plugged into a wall socket. The night-light was even brighter than the regular lamps in his room.

Cyborg flopped down on his recharging platform. He plugged himself in and settled down for a good rest.

With a jolting fizzle, the night-light sputtered and flickered out.

The room fell into total darkness.

Both Cyborg's human eye and his robot eye gleamed in the gloom. "Night-light out?" He gasped. "Lights on." He scrambled out of bed and rushed over to the light switch. "Lights on!"

Nothing happened, so Cyborg flicked the

switch up and down a dozen more times. His voice grew shriller as he chanted, "Lights on! Lights on! Lights on! Lights on!"

Finally, Cyborg gave up flicking the switch. He panted quietly in the deep darkness.

A floorboard creaked under his steel boots.

Cyborg let out a high shriek of terror. "I do not like the dark!" he hollered, bashing into furniture as he bounced around the inky dark room. "Got to find a light!" Something toppled onto the floor in a crash.

With a gasp, Cyborg spotted four sets of glowing eyes staring into the room from the dark doorway.

"Cyborg," said a growly voice. "Is everything okay?"

"We heard the screams of a small child,"

added a female, worriedly.

Cyborg shrieked again. "Eight-eyed monster!" he bellowed. Small rockets launched out
of his shoulders, exploding in the doorway in
blinding fireballs.

The detonations were followed by screams
and grunts, a whimper of pain…and then
silence in the darkness.

A few feet away, a small electric lantern lit up. Robin held the glowing lantern by its handle. Now Cyborg could see his teammates looking bedraggled, charred, and annoyed.

"Oh, phew," said Cyborg, wiping his forehead in relief. "I scared it off." He stared at his friends for a moment, taking in how blasted and smoky they were. "Wow, that monster really did a number on you guys, huh?"

His teammates glared.

"Power went out," said Robin. "I'll check the grid in the morning—"

"No!" Cyborg demanded, pointing a finger angrily in Robin's face. "You will check the grid immediately!"

The other Teen Titans glanced at one another, confused by Cyborg's overreaction.

Finally, Beast Boy transformed into a large green duck and nodded his beak thoughtfully. "Bro," he guessed, "are you scared of the dark?"

Cyborg stiffened. "Of course not!" he scoffed.

"As your friends," said Starfire sweetly, "we would understand."

Raven wiped rocket soot from her cloak. "I wouldn't," she said.

"Yeah," said Robin, agreeing with Raven. "Only babies are scared of the dark."

"I'm not scared of the dark," Cyborg insisted. He leaned down closer to Robin. His half-mechanical face lit up in the lantern light, creepy like a ghoulish mask, his human eye wide with fright. "I'm scared of what hides in it," he whispered.

"Whoa," said Beast Boy. He turned from a duck into a chicken. "Spooky."

"Right?" said Cyborg. His eyes unfocused and he shivered as he lost himself in a chilling, half-forgotten memory of his past. "It all started at a slumber party many years ago...."

CHAPTER 2

In Cyborg's memory, he was sitting on a puffy sleeping bag as a young kid, already half human, half robot. All around him was a raucous slumber party of super heroes in full force. Some kids in capes were having a pillow fight with kids in masks, feathers flying everywhere. Others danced to blaring music, wiggling their butts. Cyborg felt nervous. It was his first slumber party.

Suddenly, the music cut off. Cyborg glanced up to see all the young heroes gathered around him with surprisingly serious expressions on their faces. The light in the room had fallen into gloom.

He gulped, scared.

"My friends forced me to play Scary Teri," Cyborg explained to the Teen Titans, without letting go of the memory.

Back at the slumber party, the creepy little heroes all had pushed Cyborg into a narrow storage room. It was dark and empty in the closet, except for an ornate mirror on one wall. The kids handed him a candle and slammed the door, shutting him inside alone.

All Cyborg could see in the flickering, spooky candlelight was his own reflection in the mirror.

"That stupid baby game that's supposed to summon a scary ghost?" asked Robin.

"It's not a game," replied Cyborg. "Gathering all of my courage," he said, "I turned to the mirror and said the words." He swallowed away his dry terror. "Scary Teri. Scary Teri. Scary Teri—"

In the little storage room, Cyborg's image in the silver mirror warped and swirled.

A shocking, ghastly purple face popped into focus.

Young Cyborg screamed at the top of his mechanical lungs.

Back in Titans Tower, teen Cyborg screamed, too.

He stopped shrieking when he saw his teammates shooting him irritated looks.

Cyborg let his shoulders relax and then cleared his throat. "I barely escaped Scary Teri that night," he said softly. "That's why I've slept with a light on ever since."

A long, awkward pause followed Cyborg's explanation.

"Wow," said Robin. "That is an embarrassing story."

Beast Boy peered up at Cyborg as an otter. "You know Scary Teri isn't real, right?"

"Not real?" replied Cyborg. "She almost ate my soul. Why is this so hard to believe?" He opened his hand toward their floating, purple-and-black-clad teammate. "Raven's father is a demon!"

Raven bobbed cross-legged in the air.

"Yeah," she said, "but he doesn't waste his time hanging out at little kids' sleepovers." Her lips twitched. "Unless he's, you know, totally bored."

Cyborg had a quick vision of Raven's four-eyed, horned, bright red demon father, Trigon. He was kneeling at a slumber party, braiding a little girl's hair and giggling as they gossiped. Cyborg shook his head to clear the disturbing thought.

Robin put his hand on Cyborg's metal arm. "Maybe we can help you get over your stupid, shameful, and completely unjustified fear," he said.

"How?" asked Cyborg.

Starfire clasped her hands in excitement. "What if we held a party of slumber tonight?"

"Slumber party!" the other Titans cheered together.

The teenage teammates ran to their rooms and got dressed for the sleepover, zipping themselves into footy pajamas or other comfy sleepwear. Beast Boy turned into an elephant and grabbed his rolled-up sleeping bag in his trunk. Raven glanced around before hiding a small teddy bear in the folds of her sleep cloak. Robin fitted his teeth with orthodontic headgear, slipping the band around the back of his head.

The Titans met back up in the living room and set up their sleeping bags on the floor around Robin's lantern in front of their semicircular couch.

Raven tilted her head at Robin's headgear. "What is going on with that?" she asked.

"Part of my never-ending war on crooked

teeth," Robin replied, lisping around the metal in his mouth. "I shall never surrender!"

One of Robin's teeth decided it was time to sneak out of place. It tilted crooked, but the orthodontic appliance snagged it and yanked it violently back into proper alignment.

Robin yelped and pressed his fingers to his cheek outside the painful tooth. "Another victory," he said, wincing.

Cyborg nodded. He looked around at the sleeping bags set up around the lantern and his friends sitting in an arc around him. "So…" he said, "now we just…go to sleep?"

CHAPTER 3

"No way!" replied Beast Boy, turning into a wide-eyed owl. "Sleepovers aren't about sleeping."

"They're about all the awesome stuff you do instead of sleeping," added Raven.

Robin held up his gloved index finger. "First up," he announced, "building the world's best blanket fort…" He flipped open a large blanket, unfurling it wide.

"Yeah!" the other Titans cheered. "Woo!"

Robin pulled out a page of complicated schematics. "According to these very detailed blueprints I made!" he finished.

His teammates heaved grumbling sighs.

Robin smoothed out the blueprints on the floor. "We'll start with laying the foundation," he explained. "Then, in two hours, when that's done, we can…"

He trailed off as he saw that the other Teen Titans were staring at him in dismay.

"Oh, come on," argued Robin. "It's not that complicated, once the primary support column is up—"

Nobody else reacted. They held their

expressions of blank disapproval.

Robin rolled his eyes. "I'll do it myself." He plopped a hard hat on his head, took the corner of the big blanket, and got to work.

"Hey, Cyborg?" asked Beast Boy, his voice impish. "Know the best part about slumber parties?" He turned into a green gorilla. "Pillow fight!" Beast Boy let out a war cry as he launched at Cyborg with his pillow raised for the attack.

Starfire swooped in to intercept Beast Boy. She swatted him down with her pillow. Cyborg joined Starfire in smacking Beast Boy with their pillows until he was pummeled into a heap on the floor.

"Raven, help!" cried Beast Boy. "I'm under attack!"

Raven hovered cross-legged a few inches

above her pillow on the floor. She flipped a page in the book she was reading. "No, thanks."

Cyborg gave Beast Boy another good whack on the head.

"Raven, c'mon!"

"I'm not playing," replied Raven.

Beast Boy popped up as a cute puppy with big pleading eyes. "Aw, please?" he begged Raven. "It won't be fun if you don't play!"

Starfire, Cyborg, and Beast Boy held their pillows over their heads. "Pillow fight!" they chanted. "Pillow fight! Pillow fight!"

Raven frowned. Without even giving her teammates a sideways glance, she conjured purplish dark-magic tentacles. The squidlike arms wriggled and snatched the pillows out of the other Titans' grasps. Then the tentacles whacked Starfire, Cyborg, and Beast Boy on the head until they were smashed and lay crushed and defeated on the ground.

"There," said Raven. "Happy?"

After they had all recovered from the pillow fight, Starfire, Beast Boy, Cyborg, and Raven fluffed their pillows and arranged their sleeping bags in a close, cozy circle. Behind them, Robin flipped down a welding mask and lit up the brilliant blue concentrated flame of a gas torch. Then he bent over out of view, constructing his blanket tent.

Cyborg sat down in the circle of sleeping bags. He smiled at Starfire and Beast Boy. "I'm starting to feel better about the dark—"

He jumped, startled and scared. "Oh my goodness, it's a demon!" he squealed. "A demon!" Cyborg had only caught a glimpse of Raven out of the corner of his eye. He cowered beside her.

"Really?" Raven asked. She fixed him with a level gaze as she bobbed in the air above her black sleeping bag.

"You float there like a ghost," said Cyborg, sitting up. "What do you want from me?"

"Oooh, Titans!" chirped Starfire, changing the subject. "I know an activity to take

Cyborg's mind off his fear: the game of candor or audacious undertaking!"

Beast Boy, Cyborg, and Raven blinked at Starfire blankly.

CHAPTER 4

"You mean truth or dare," realized Raven.

"Ohhhh," said Beast Boy and Cyborg, nodding their heads.

Starfire batted her eyelashes. "Who knows what crazy things I might do if given the dare!"

With a whooshing sound, Robin appeared in the circle, bumping Beast Boy to the side.

He gazed hopefully at Starfire. "I dare you to kiss—" He gasped. "No! I dare you to date me for a few years, and then move in with me, and then one night, when the moon is full, to watch me bend one down on one knee…"

Cyborg blanked out for a while, weirded out by Robin's dare overshare. When he focused back in again, Robin was still going.

"…and to name our third child Carrie,

after my favorite aunt…" Robin recited.

Cyborg mentally left town again. He only came back to the bizarre monologue when it sounded like Robin was winding down.

"…then to hold my hand as the sun goes down over the mountains and whisper in my ear, 'It's been a good life,'" Robin finished. "That is your dare."

A long, uncomfortable silence hung over the slumber party in the aftermath of Robin's dare.

"I was going to pick the truth," said Starfire.

"Oh," said Robin. He smiled at Starfire nervously. "Would you do all that stuff?"

Starfire winced. "No."

"I see," said Robin. His back and shoulders slumped. He pointed his thumb behind him. "I'll be in the blanket fort."

Robin got up and shuffled into his fort, vanishing into its draped blankets.

The other Titans sat in their circle, grimacing as they listened to Robin moan within the tent.

"Why, Robin, why?" he sobbed, though muffled by the fort walls. "You *had* to put it all out there. Stupid! Stupid! She thinks you're a jerk! Why doesn't she love me? My teeth are straight! They're so straight...." His voice collapsed into weeping.

Cyborg sat up straight and smiled. "Oh!" he said. "I got a good dare!"

In no time, the Titans snuck out into the moonlit night. They crept to a certain mansion...and hurled eggs at the gargoyles on its roof.

The front door opened with a loud creak.

Batman, wearing a fancy robe over his costume, appeared in the rectangle of yellow light spilling out. He glared into the darkness.

"Oh no!" hissed Cyborg. "It's old man Batman. Run!"

The Titans scattered, scrambling back to the Tower.

"Woo!" said Cyborg as they settled down in their slumber party circle again. "That was fun!"

Beast Boy transformed into a parrot. "That's what I'm talking about, bro!"

"Are you feeling better about the night-time?" asked Starfire.

"You know what?" replied Cyborg. He settled back onto his sleeping bag. "I think I am!"

The other Titans wriggled into their

sleeping bags, getting comfortable.

Robin smiled sincerely at Cyborg. "I'm glad you decided to stop acting like a big dumb baby," he said. "Well, good night."

He turned off his electric lantern.

The room fell into darkness.

Cyborg sat up, screaming his head off. He launched rockets again, blasting the entire living room...and everyone in it.

The other Titans groaned in pain.

Robin clicked the lantern back on.

The room was toast. The couch had been blasted backward, and it smoldered with low, smoky fires. The Titans were blackened and charred, their sleeping bags exploded and ruined.

"Everybody safe?" asked Cyborg. "Pretty sure I heard Scary Teri."

His teammates glared furiously at him.

"Okay," Robin growled. "I think there's only one way to fix this."

Raven, Starfire, and Beast Boy nodded solemnly. They all got up and closed in on Cyborg, who took a step backward.

"What are you—" said Cyborg, raising his hands in defense. "No. C'mon, you wouldn't...."

CHAPTER 5

Cyborg's teammates shoved him, armed with only a flickering candle for light, into a dark room with a mirror, and they shut him inside.

"I don't want to play Scary Teri," protested Cyborg, his voice tinged with panic.

"Just do it, Cyborg," insisted Robin.

"You guys don't understand," cried Cyborg. "She'll destroy us all!"

"Say it first," Robin demanded.

Cyborg shook his head, staring into the candle flame. He took a deep breath, gathering his courage. Then, in a rush, he shouted, "Scary Teri! Scary Teri! Scary Teri!"

Robin leaned close to his side of the door. "See, Cyborg?" he called. "Isn't that better—?"

The door exploded outward. Cyborg tumbled out, smashing into his teammates and knocking them to the floor in a heap.

A purple ghoul with a shock of white hair floated through the smashed doorway. Scary Teri wore only tattered rags. She bared her sharp, ghostly teeth, raising her arms to threaten the Titans.

The Teen Titans screamed, huddling together in terror.

"What did I tell you?" moaned Cyborg.

"She's so scary!" cried Robin, ducking his head.

Scary Teri let out a vicious hiss.

Beast Boy turned into a tiny mouse. "Her ragged clothes!" he squeaked.

Scary Teri dropped her arms and peered down at her shredded garments. "I just bought these," she said.

Starfire shuddered. "Her ratty, unkempt hair!"

"I didn't have time to wash it this morning," said Scary Teri, patting her head.

"Her dirty, ugly face," Raven added.

Scary Teri frowned, insulted. "This is just how I look."

"Oh," said Robin.

"Sorry," said Raven.

"No, you're right," replied Scary Teri. "I should really take care better care of myself." She emitted a heinous, blood-chilling shriek as she shriveled and stretched into a huge, horrifying, hideous demon skeleton with long white hair.

The Titans screamed and fled into the living room.

"How do we defeat her?" asked Raven.

Cyborg glared at Raven. "Wow, that's a weird way of saying, 'Oh, Cyborg, you were totally right. Sorry for making you relive your childhood trauma.'" The blank looks of all his teammates made him drop his scolding. "We need a mirror," he replied.

"I have several full-length and handheld

mirrors in my room," said Robin.

Beast Boy turned into an eagle and looked down the hallway. "But she's blocking Robin's room," he reported.

"To the blanket fort!" Robin declared. "Go, go, go!" He rushed toward the entrance to his tent.

With a shrug, Raven followed Robin, and the rest of the Titans hurried after her. They ducked into the folds of the fort's entry tunnel seconds before Scary Teri, still a terrifying skeleton creature, wandered into the living room.

The Titans crawled through a narrow tunnel of blankets, scrambling toward the interior of Robin's fort.

"Did you seriously put a mirror in here?"

asked Raven as she crawled.

"Among other things," replied Robin.

Robin climbed out of the tunnel, standing up. His teammates gathered around him in the foyer of a magnificent mansion inside the blankets. A grand staircase swept upward to a higher floor, a chandelier dangled from the fabric ceiling, and a pretty little fountain burbled in the center of the entry chamber.

The Titans gasped and murmured, wowed by Robin's handiwork.

"Is that a basketball court?" Beast Boy asked. He turned into a giraffe and craned his long neck to peek down the hall of blankets.

"No," said Robin. "That's the bowling alley. The basketball court is in the basement."

"Cool!" cheered Beast Boy.

"Yeah, yeah," said Cyborg. "It's impressive."

An enormous crash outside the fort shook the blanket walls.

"But there's a demon lady trying to eat our souls!" yelled Cyborg.

With another bone-jarring thud and the sound of tearing fabric, Scary Teri ripped her way through the fort ceiling. She had transformed into a massive pterodactyl with demon eyes, and she screeched in evil triumph.

CHAPTER 6

Scary Teri dropped through the ceiling. She changed on her way down into a gargantuan lump of flesh with tiny arms and legs. Her mouth took up most of her grotesque body, and she lashed out with her long tongue at the Titans.

Robin, Starfire, Raven, and Beast Boy were trapped behind her, cornered in the fort.

Only Cyborg had access to any exits.

"Cyborg," called Robin around Scary Teri. "You have to get the mirror. It's in the second guest bedroom." He pointed to a murky doorway across the room.

"But—but—it's dark," whined Cyborg. "Scary Teri could be in there."

Scary Teri screeched again as she whipped her long tongue closer to his teammates.

"Scary Teri's right here, dude!" hollered Beast Boy.

Then Scary Teri snagged Beast Boy with her tongue, wrapping it six times around his squirming green body.

Beast Boy screamed in horror.

The mirror demon yanked him into her vast open mouth and devoured him.

"Beast Boy!" cried Starfire.

Cyborg tightened his hands to fists. "Okay," he said, setting his metal jaw in determination. "I can do this." He marched through the dark doorway and disappeared into the gloom beyond.

Moments after he'd entered the room, Cyborg let out a shout in the darkness. The tinkle of shattering glass chimed in the fort. Cyborg came running back into the front hall, his hands empty.

"I couldn't do it," he panted. "I'm sorry."

Scary Teri smiled. Then she lassoed Starfire with her tongue and gulped her down. Starfire's scream was cut off as Scary Teri swallowed her.

"There's another mirror in the second-floor rumpus room," Robin told Cyborg. "Go!"

Cyborg nodded. "Got it," he said. He sprinted up the stairs…into another pitch black room. This time, he only lasted seconds before hollering in horror as the sound of breaking glass echoed everywhere. He ran out again.

"I thought it would help if I closed my eyes, but I just tripped," he explained.

Raven screamed as Scary Teri lapped her up with her tongue and chomped her down.

"Look," Robin said, trying to stay calm although he was terrified and desperate. "There's one more mirror. First-floor dining room. You can do it. Just because you're scared doesn't mean you're not strong—"

Robin couldn't finish his sentence. Scary Teri ate him.

"Mmm," said Scary Teri, licking her giant blubbery lips. "Scared souls. So tasty." She faced Cyborg, her eyes glowing hungrily at him. "You're next, little boy!"

Cyborg cringed back. But then he opened his human eye. It wasn't filled with fear. It glinted with steely courage....Then something snapped. He stared her down.

"I'm not a little boy anymore," he yelled at Scary Teri.

Cyborg ran, shrieking like a frightened child. He dashed past Scary Teri, ducking under a swipe of her sticky tongue. Cyborg rolled across the fortress floor, hopping to his feet at another dark doorway. With a deep breath, he charged inside.

A split second later, he ran out again with a small pink hand mirror in his grip.

Cyborg held the mirror up to Scary Teri.

"Scary Teri isn't scary," Cyborg chanted. "Scary Teri isn't scary. Scary Teri isn't scary!"

The silver surface of the mirror swirled. A churning portal opened into another dimension. With a whooshing sound, the portal vacuumed Scary Teri toward its vortex.

"No!" shrieked Scary Teri. She grabbed the blanket walls, struggling against the mirror's sucking pull, but the fabric tore. The blankets ripped apart, pillows toppled down everywhere, as Scary Teri vanished into the whirlpool in the mirror. The fort tumbled down, collapsing in the living room of Titans Tower.

When the dust had settled, the blankets squirmed. Cyborg flipped the bedding off him. The other Titans lay around him, coughing but free from Scary Teri's stomach.

"Ha!" said Cyborg, pumping his fist. "I finally got you, you scary witch. Best sleepover ever!"

His teammates cheered...before collapsing into coughing again.

That night, Cyborg yawned as he plodded into his bedroom. He lay down on his recharging platform. "Bedtime," he muttered. "Lights out."

Cyborg clicked off his light.

His little night-light glowed nearby.

Cyborg turned off the night-light, too.

A moment later, Cyborg whispered in the darkness, "Scary Teri. Scary Teri. Scary Teri."

CHAPTER

1

The Teen Titans gathered at Robin's request on the roof of Titans Tower. Robin stood in front of a large, squarish object covered by a tarp.

"Titans!" exclaimed Robin. "Exciting news! I've just installed a heated hydrotherapy chamber!" He leaned toward his teammates, expecting them to cheer.

Starfire, Raven, and Cyborg merely blinked blankly at the Boy Wonder.

Beast Boy turned into a sloth and hung from an air-conditioning vent, yawning. "Not exciting, bro," he muttered.

Robin smiled. "Would you be more excited if I told you it was a..." With a magician's flourish, he whipped off the tarp.

Underneath was a steaming whirlpool bath filled with bubbling water.

"Hot tub!" squealed Starfire. She raced toward the water, with Raven and Beast Boy right behind her.

"Now, wait," Robin protested, "the hydrotherapy chamber is only for post-training soreness—"

Raven and Starfire hopped into the tub, luxuriating in its soothing, burbling heat.

"Let us do the time of the party in a large container of warm water!" Starfire sighed. "The jets feel like tiny *florthogs* nibbling at your *norbobs*!"

Raven laughed, low and mellow. "Bubbles," she said.

"Everyone out!" Robin ordered. "The tub is for—"

Robin didn't get to finish his sentence, because Beast Boy launched himself into the tub, transforming into a hippopotamus before he hit the water. A giant splash drenched Robin.

"Hot tub!" Beast Boy bellowed.

Soaked and grumpy, Robin turned around to look at Cyborg, who hadn't moved. "At least you respect my orders," Robin said.

"Oh, it's not that," replied Cyborg. "It's not that at all. It's because I"—his human eye narrowed—"can't"—his robot eye flashed red—"enjoy"—Cyborg tightened his metal hands into steely fists—"hot tubs!" he hollered.

All his teammates gasped in surprise and dismay.

"A robot body is great for a lot of things," Cyborg explained. "Looking real shiny. Hacking Robin's very personal data files—"

"I'm sorry?" interjected Robin.

"And being real, real, real tough," continued Cyborg. "But enjoying the warm, bubbly embrace of a hot tub just isn't one of them." His shoulders slumped and he heaved a deep sigh. "Sometimes I wish I were a real boy again. But I've searched the world, and there's simply nobody who can—"

Raven popped her wet head out of the tub. "I can do that," she said.

Cyborg blinked at her. "Excuse me?"

CHAPTER 2

"I can make you human again," Raven told Cyborg. "Because, you know, magic."

Instantly, Cyborg reached into the hot tub and pulled Raven up in a hug.

She endured his embrace patiently.

"Why didn't you ever say anything before?" Cyborg asked.

Raven shrugged. "Come on," she said. "It

would take way too long to list everything I can do with magic."

Beast Boy turned into an elephant, and he held out one giant ear. "We want to hear the list!"

The other Teen Titans turned toward Raven, waiting.

Raven rolled her eyes. "Ugh, fine," she said, and she began to recite her magical skills. "Teleportation. Telekinesis. Flight. Read the minds of animals. See in the dark. Turn water into any other liquid except for ginger ale…"

It took nearly four days for Raven to get through the entire list of what her magical powers could accomplish. Her teammates, enrapt, listened the whole time. Finally, she reached the last few items.

"Summon a meteor," she continued, her

voice gravelly from talking nonstop for so long. "Devour the souls of the wicked. And… perfectly crack open walnuts."

Beast Boy transformed into a green toucan. "Walnuts are hard to open," he said, impressed.

"Okay, enough yammering," said Cyborg. "I got some hot tubbing to do!"

That night, Raven prepared her mystical enchantment in the Titans' yard. She drew arcane symbols on the ground, with flickering candles glowing at the points of most intense energy. Starfire, Beast Boy, and Robin watched respectfully from the sidelines. Magic could be so dangerous!

Cyborg lay in the center of the symbols, looking nervous and excited. "Is this going to hurt?" he asked.

"Nope," replied Raven. "I won't feel a thing."

Cyborg glared at her.

"Ha," said Raven. "And you guys say I'm not funny."

None of the other Titans changed their expressions at all.

"But seriously," Raven continued, "this will be extremely painful."

Before Cyborg could even gulp, Raven threw her head back, and chanted, "*Azarath Metrion Zinthos!*"

Glowing beams of black-and-purple magical energy shot from Raven's outstretched hands. The radiating power surrounded Cyborg, wrapping him up in a cocoon of dark force. He wriggled as he floated a few feet off the ground.

Then Cyborg let out a horrible scream, and he writhed in pain. "The agony!" he cried. "The agonizingly agonizing agony!"

In a blinding flash of power, Raven completed her magical spell.

The robot parts of Cyborg's body pulled free from his human form, falling to the ground with metallic clunks and thunks.

Cyborg twisted in the air and turned upright. His feet lowered, until he was standing on his own.

Without his metal armor shell, he was completely human.

And completely naked.

His teammates covered their eyes and screamed.

Raven quickly handed Cyborg a towel.

He covered himself, and the other Titans sighed in relief.

Cyborg stared down at his body, which was entirely healthy flesh. His eyes were bright with amazement and happiness, and he laughed with pure joy.

"You did it," he breathed. "I'm human again."

CHAPTER 3

Raven nodded in acknowledgment of Cyborg's thanks, hovering cross-legged in the air beside him. "Now, I have to warn you," she said, "your human nervous system is very sensitive compared to your robot body—"

Cyborg laughed. "All I'm hearing is *hot tub hot hot hot hot tub!*" He sprinted toward the tub and leaped into the bubbling water.

Immediately, he popped up again, screaming in pain. "I'm being cooked alive!" he screeched.

He clawed his way over the edge of the whirlpool bath, and flopped, steaming, flat on the roof.

After he had cooled a bit, Cyborg moaned, "Why was the hot tub so hot?"

"Because you're human," replied Raven, "and humans feel way more pain than robots."

"Yeah," Robin agreed. "Sorry, Cyborg, but it's—" He froze with his mouth open, realizing something important. "Hang on," he said. "Wow, we can't even call you Cyborg anymore, can we?"

Cyborg raised his head off the ground. "You can't?"

Beast Boy turned into a blubbery manatee

and peeked at Cyborg from the hot tub. "Yeah, bro," he said, "you're just a fleshy guy now." A smile lit up Beast Boy's whiskered face. "Fleshy Guy!" he exclaimed. "That can be your new name! Man, I'm so great at naming things."

Cyborg squinted. "I'm not sure I want to be—"

"Fleshy Guy," repeated Robin, rubbing his chin.

"The Fleshy…" said Starfire, testing the name uncertainly. "Guy."

Raven floated down to Fleshy Guy's level and tilted to peer at him. "You don't want to be a cyborg again, do you?" she asked.

"No," Fleshy Guy, formerly Cyborg, replied. "I just have a lot to learn about being a real boy. That's all."

"That's the spirit, Fleshy Guy!" said Beast Boy. He transformed into a little cricket and hopped on his friend's shoulder. "I'll be your guide to being a human! Just follow me."

Over the next few hours, Beast Boy tutored Fleshy Guy on the basics of being fully human. He helped his teammate get dressed in jeans and a T-shirt and taught him very important lessons about bones, reflexes, shoes, and, especially, deodorant.

In the kitchen of Titans Tower, Beast Boy opened the refrigerator. "You still like food?" he asked over his shoulder. "Well, you're going to love it even more, Fleshy Guy!" He started tossing out snacks.

Fleshy Guy grabbed the food and gobbled it down frighteningly fast. He laughed maniacally. "These snacks taste so much better in my human belly!"

"That's what I'm saying, Fleshy Guy," Beast Boy replied. He turned into a squid so he could use his tentacles to clean out the fridge faster. When the fridge was empty, he moved on to the dry goods pantry.

Fleshy Guy kept eating like a garbage truck. "This is so good!" he cried, crunching a mouthful of dry pasta. He coughed out a puff of orange powdered cheese.

Beast Boy grinned. "If you think that's

good," he said, "wait until you try this!" He pressed a hidden button on the wall, and the kitchen shuddered and echoed with a grinding noise.

A secret hatch in the kitchen table slowly slid open as the lights dimmed in the room. Clouds of smoke issued out of a hole in the table as a mysterious, shadowy object rose into view on a platform.

"Once every three hundred years," Beast Boy explained, "all the major food groups align in the cosmos." He opened the refrigerator door, and the low light from the fridge lit the smoke around Beast Boy dramatically. He raised his tentacles and chanted, "Taco, burger, hot dog, pizza!" The smoke began to clear. "All coming together as one to form…"

The kitchen lights flashed on brightly, revealing a heap of mixed-up food dripping with cheese and grease on the table.

"El Burdigato Supreme!" shouted Beast Boy.

Fleshy Guy started to drool uncontrollably.

CHAPTER 4

In the blink of an eye, Fleshy Guy had consumed the massive jumble of food. He tottered into the living room and slumped onto the couch, his stomach swollen and achingly full.

"My human belly," groaned Fleshy Guy.

Transforming into a cricket again, Beast Boy jumped onto Fleshy Guy's arm. He stared down at his teammate's pulsating stomach. "Huh," he chirped. "Maybe we overdid it. Just a little."

Fleshy Guy shot Beast Boy an annoyed look, but then his stomach rumbled horribly. He cradled his tummy with his arms. "What was that?"

"That is the Burdigato," replied Beast Boy.

Then Fleshy Guy's stomach growled again, this time much louder and angrier. He hoisted himself to his feet, his eyes wide and worried. "Uh-oh," he muttered. He rushed down the hall toward the bathroom.

A moment later, Beast Boy's communicator buzzed.

"Hey, Beastie," Fleshy Guy whispered over the communicator. "Uh…can you come in for a sec?"

"Why?" Beast Boy asked, laughing softly. "You need help?" The human Beast Boy walked down the hall and entered the bathroom.

When Beast Boy got a look at what was going on in the bathroom, his eyes nearly bugged out of his head. He covered his mouth in horror, and then uncovered it to holler, "What are you doing with your feet in there?"

Fleshy Guy blushed in embarrassment. "It's been a while since I've used one of these, okay?" he replied.

By the time they had gotten that mess cleaned up, Fleshy Guy felt much better, and it was time for bed.

Beast Boy, back to being a cricket, curled up to sleep on Fleshy Guy's shoulder as his friend tried to get comfortable on the stiff slab he had used to rest and recharge while he was a cyborg.

"Great first day, Fleshy Guy," Beast Boy said sleepily. "Isn't being a human awesome?"

Fleshy Guy twitched on his slab, shifting awkwardly, his limbs flopping with weariness. "Why…is it so hard…to move my body?" he asked.

Beast Boy opened one cricket eye, looking a little annoyed that Fleshy Guy's wiggling was keeping him up. "Because you're tired, dude," he replied. "Happens to all of us. You just need to recharge your batteries!"

"That I can do," said Fleshy Guy. He reached up, grabbed the electric helmet that hung over his slab, and pulled it down onto his head. It switched on automatically, blasting sizzling bolts of voltage into Fleshy Guy's human brain.

Fleshy Guy screamed in shocked pain.

Beast Boy nodded, chuckling. "I can see where you might have misunderstood me," he said.

The next morning, Fleshy Guy dragged himself out of bed. Beast Boy was already up and gone, and Fleshy Guy could hear the low voices of his teammates talking from the kitchen. He barely had the energy to stand up, but he stumbled and weaved out of his room and padded down the hall barefoot into the kitchen.

Raven, Robin, Starfire, and Beast Boy were perched on stools at the kitchen counter, eating cereal with comic books open beside their bowls.

"Good morning, the Fleshy Guy!" said Starfire.

Fleshy Guy shaded his eyes with his hand as he wobbled by the counter.

"Ah," said Raven, "you decided to sleep in, huh?"

"Sleep in?" Fleshy Guy protested. "I barely slept at all. This human body keeps sloshing around and making weird noises."

He slid onto a stool and pulled a comic book closer to himself. "Today I just want to relax and read comics," he said, picking it up by its edge. "Ow!" he cried, holding up a bleeding finger.

"What happened?"

"That is a cut of the paper," Starfire explained with a shudder. "It happens to those of us without metal hands."

Fleshy Guy sucked the tip of his finger. "Well," he said, "I don't like it." He stood up to leave, and stubbed his toe on the leg of the stool. "Ow!" he screamed, hopping.

"Got to watch those toes, bro," said Beast Boy.

"What is wrong with your weird soft bodies?" Fleshy Guy yelled. "I can't take this anymore!" He burst into tears and dashed out of the kitchen, sobbing.

"Poor the Fleshy Guy," sighed Starfire. "I feel sad about his sad."

Beast Boy started to slide off his stool as a giant slug. "Maybe I should go check on him."

"No," Robin said. "This is a real-boy problem." He stood up, staring pointedly at Beast Boy's slimy green slug body. "It should be handled by…a real boy."

CHAPTER

5

In his room, Fleshy Guy stood before his closet, staring at the various metallic suits he used to wear as Cyborg. With a deep sigh, he pulled out one of his sets of everyday robot armor and held it up to his chest.

It glinted beautifully in the light.

Fleshy Guy tried to fit the arm piece around his human arm, but it wouldn't stay attached.

He struggled with it, getting more and more upset—

A knock on the door made him whirl around, his eyes red with anger and tears.

"Hey," said Robin, peeking around the doorframe, "is there a real boy in here that needs cheering up?"

Fleshy Guy didn't reply. Instead, he refocused on getting his metal suit onto his human body.

"Hey, hey," Robin said, gently calming Fleshy Guy down before he hurt himself. "Being a human boy isn't that bad, you know."

"Are you kidding?" replied Fleshy Guy. "It's horrible! I can't imagine anybody living a single day like this—"

He suddenly realized that he was talking to

Robin. Who had always been totally human.

"Oh, right," Fleshy Guy said, staring at the floor. "Sorry."

Robin shrugged, not particularly insulted. "Sure, we humans can't fly," he said, "or lift cars or reach the top shelf without a stepladder—"

Fleshy Guy raised an eyebrow at that. "I can still reach it just fine," he said. He looked Robin up and down. "You're short."

Robin frowned but forged ahead, ignoring the mild insult. "There are plenty of really awesome things about being human," he continued. "So go back to being a robot if you want. But first," he said, slinging his arm around Fleshy Guy's shoulders, "let me take you on a Real-Boy Adventure!"

The next hours were filled with Robin leading Fleshy Guy on a celebration of the joys of having a human body. They ate delicious food, listened to cool music, took relaxing hot-tub baths, and worked out in the Titans Tower gym.

Then Robin took Fleshy Guy to the airport for the next part of their adventure. Fleshy Guy was amazed that he could walk through the security metal detector without setting off the alarms!

Robin and Fleshy Guy flew to the Rocky Mountains, where they skied and sledded and wrote their names in the high-altitude snow…with a water gun.

Next stop on their adventure was the coast, where Fleshy Guy and Robin hit the beach.

They jumped around in the ocean, surfed, and then relaxed on the sand to soak up some rays.

Laughing, the two beach boys slapped their bare bellies, grooving to their awesome rhythms.

They kept up that same rhythm as they danced that night under streetlamps in the rain.

Robin and Fleshy Guy ducked into a concert hall, where Batman was up onstage. Batman blew everyone away with an insane guitar solo, rocking out to a crowd of real boys.

Exhausted but happy from their Real-Boy Adventure, Fleshy Guy and Robin returned home to Titans Tower.

The first thing Fleshy Guy did was collect all his robot parts in a box. He carried the collection through the living room, where his teammates were chilling out. "Man, I never knew what I was missing as a robot," he said, showing his friends the box of parts. "Guess I don't need these anymore."

Robin smiled as Fleshy Guy dumped the metal armor down the trash chute.

That's when an alarm rang through the Tower. Warning lights flashed along the walls.

"Crime alert," growled Robin.

Starfire ran over to a monitor and checked the readout, with Raven peering over her shoulder. "The alarm," said Starfire, "it is coming from—"

"The pool?" said Raven, pointing on the monitor at the Tower roof.

Beast Boy's mouth dropped open in horror. "Our hot tub is getting stolen!"

CHAPTER 6

Fleshy Guy, Beast Boy, Raven, and Starfire rushed upstairs to their rooftop pool. They immediately recognized the robbers carrying away their hot tub. They were Mammoth, Jinx, and Gizmo, three of their archenemies from the H.I.V.E. Five! Well… Mammoth was doing most of the heavy lifting.

"Drop the hot tub, creeps!" Fleshy Guy ordered.

Mammoth put down the whirlpool bath. He, Jinx, and Gizmo faced off against Fleshy Guy, Beast Boy, Raven, and Starfire by the edge of the roof.

Gizmo peered at the team through his green goggles. "Whoa," he said. "Cyborg, what happened?"

"Cyborg's gone," replied Fleshy Guy. "I'm...Fleshy Guy!" He struck a heroic pose, flexing his impressive human muscles.

Robin cleared his throat behind Fleshy Guy. "I think he was talking to me," he said.

Everybody whirled around to look at Robin, who was wearing Cyborg's old metal armor!

"Booyah!" Robin cheered.

129

Beast Boy turned into a dog and tilted his head quizzically. "Robin?" he asked. "What are you doing?"

"You heard me," Robin said. "Booyah!"

"Stop saying my catchphrase," insisted Fleshy Guy.

"Sorry," Robin said with a clanking shrug. "It's my catchphrase now. Comes with the suit."

Confused, Fleshy Guy stepped toward Robin. "So...the Real-Boy Adventure," he said, his voice surprised and hurt, "the skiing, the beach, the dancing, the tummy thumping...was all that just to get my robot parts?"

"Uh...yeah," replied Robin. "Why would I ever be human when I can have rocket boots?"

Robin reached down and pressed a button on the metal footwear. "Rocket boots!" he hollered.

But corkscrews and pinwheels and a fishing rod popped out instead.

"Uh, sorry," said Robin. "Still working out some of the bugs." He stomped his boots and turned to face the three villains. "Now,

H.I.V.E.," he growled, "prepare to—"

The rockets in Robin's boots ignited. He screamed as he was blasted sideways on jets of fire. Tumbling out of control, he knocked Beast Boy, Raven, and Starfire off the side of the roof with him. They all shrieked as they fell out of view.

Only Fleshy Guy remained standing by the hot tub.

Mammoth, Jinx, and Gizmo glared at Fleshy Guy. Mammoth punched his palm as they stepped closer menacingly.

Fleshy Guy stepped back. "Don't hurt me," he protested. "I'm just a weak little human...."

Then Fleshy Guy realized something important. He might be human, but that didn't mean he was weak! Just because he was no longer mostly metal didn't make him less of a hero. He narrowed his eyes in determination and planted his feet solidly on the rooftop.

"Just like you," he said.

In a flash, Fleshy Guy whipped a series of comic books at Jinx. Each one sliced her with nasty paper cuts. "Sorry," he said. "Put some ice on that."

Out of the corner of his eye, Fleshy Guy saw Mammoth charging toward him. Rather than run or avoid the attack, Fleshy Guy turned and barreled right toward the giant villain.

Before they smashed together, Fleshy Guy dropped down into a slide...and kicked Mammoth in the toe.

Mammoth bellowed in pain. He hopped on one foot, holding his injured toe.

"Ha!" laughed Fleshy Guy.

Gizmo activated one of his gadgets. Long spindly spider legs poked out of his backpack, raising him up for a dangerous attack. Those legs had sharp points!

Fleshy Guy ducked and rolled, dodging the spiked spider legs. Then he whirled around, grabbed Gizmo, and tossed the little villain into the hot tub.

"Ah!" Gizmo screeched, his spider legs waving in pain. "Too hot! Too hot in the hot tub!"

As Starfire and Raven carried Robin back onto the roof, and Beast Boy flew up as an eagle, Fleshy Guy admired his work defeating the H.I.V.E. all alone with no robotic armor.

Fleshy Guy raised his shirt and slapped his belly in a musical rhythm of power and victory. "Now that's what I call a Real-Boy Adventure!"

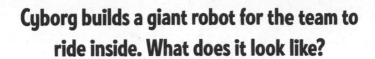

Cyborg builds a giant robot for the team to ride inside. What does it look like?

Read all the
TEEN TITANS GO! books.